Tilly and the Rhinoceros

Sheila White Samton

PHILOMEL BOOKS   NEW YORK

This story is dedicated to the memory of my father, Morris White, and the future of my sons, Joshua and Matthew Samton.

SWS

Copyright © 1993 by Sheila White Samton
Published by Philomel Books, a division of The Putnam & Grosset Group,
200 Madison Avenue, New York, NY 10016. All rights reserved.
This book, or parts thereof, may not be reproduced in any form
without permission in writing from the publisher.
Published simultaneously in Canada.
Printed in Hong Kong by South China Printing Co. (1988), Ltd.
Lettering by Sheila White Samton. The text is set in Trump Medieval.
Sheila Samton painted sheets of rice paper with acrylic, gouache, and
watercolor paints, and added black ink line. She then cut out shapes
from the prepared rice paper to create the illustrations for this book.

Library of Congress Cataloging-in-Publication Data
Samton, Sheila White.
Tilly and the rhinoceros / written and illustrated by Sheila White Samton.
  p. cm. Summary: By her sweet and caring ways, Tilly the goose turns
a grumpy rhinoceros who threatens the economic life of the village into a
delightful, helpful friend to all.
[1. Geese—Fiction. 2. Rhinoceros—Fiction.] I. Title.
PZ7.S185Ti 1933 [E]—dc20 92-2654 CIP AC
ISBN 0-399-21973-0

10 9 8 7 6 5 4 3 2 1

First Impression

Everyone loved Tilly Gobble, the tiniest goose in the neighborhood.

If you were sick, she came and read to you.

If you were hurt, she bandaged your wounds.

And she always remembered the sad and lonely on Saint Valentine's Day. When a goose is your friend, she is your friend for life.

Tilly made feather pillows and feather quilts and feather hats. Every Monday she took her wares to the market and came home with everything she needed for the rest of the week, and lots of things her friends needed, too.

But one crisp morning, when the leaves were changing color, Tilly went to the market and discovered a huge rhinoceros lying across the road. His big body blocked the way to the market and the prince's castle next door.

Tilly just watched, as other marketgoers began to arrive. A baker with a tray of cupcakes was the first to approach the rhinoceros.

"Excuse me, your Mightiness," the baker mumbled nervously. "May we go by?"

"Certainly!" barked the dangerous-looking beast. "If you can answer my riddle: What grows higher as it comes down?"

"Is it yeast?" asked the baker.

"No!" yelled the rhinoceros. "What a dumb answer! You can't go by!" He grabbed the tray and spilled the cupcakes down his huge throat.

"Is it a sunflower?" a florist with a wagonload of bouquets spoke up.

"Ha, ha, ha! No, it's not!" bellowed the rhinoceros. "Even a hippo would have a better answer! You can't go by, either!" He grabbed a bouquet and began to eat the delicate blossoms, one by one.

All day long the marketgoers tried to answer the riddle and failed. When the sun set they finally turned around and went home, still carrying the things they had hoped to sell. Tilly went home, too.

Through the night many countryfolk stayed awake, trying to solve the riddle. Tilly was also awake. But she was not trying to solve the riddle. She was wondering how it felt to sleep on the hard road without a pillow.

Morning finally came, and the rhinoceros was still there. And still, no one could answer the riddle.

Time went by. In Tilly's cottage, the quilts and pillows and hats piled up until there was hardly room for Tilly and no room for visitors.

In the apple orchards, the fruit began to rot. In the mills, sacks of flour lay stacked, waiting to be baked into bread. All over the land milk and butter spoiled, eggs spilled out of coops, and mountains of shoes grew up around cobblers' benches.

Still, no one could answer the riddle.

Finally, in despair, the prince offered a reward: five hundred golden rubles for the right answer, plus his extra castle with a swimming pool. He hung out of the window, wondering if the lucky winner would be any of the countryfolk below him.

Still, no one could answer the riddle. The situation seemed hopeless.

The days grew chilly, and visitors scarce. One afternoon the rhinoceros saw a tiny goose coming up the road. It was Tilly, carrying a large feather pillow.

"Hi!" he roared at her. "What grows higher as it comes down?"

"I don't know," said Tilly.

"Too bad," boomed the rhinoceros. "But it doesn't matter. There's no market here anymore. Nobody can answer my riddle. Ha, ha! Give that pillow to some old granny."

"It's for you," said Tilly. "May you sleep soundly on this cold, hard road." And she tucked the pillow behind the rhinoceros's head.

For the first time in his life, the rhinoceros was speechless. No one had ever given him a present for being a mean bully. He made a noise like "mooph" that Tilly took to mean "thank you." "Don't mention it," she said.

A week later Tilly came again. It was a bitter evening, and the road was icy under her webbed feet.

"Hi!" thundered the rhinoceros. "What grows higher as it comes down?"

"I'm afraid I still don't know," confessed Tilly. "But here's a quilt to keep you warm." She unfurled a fluffy feather quilt and settled it around him.

At first the rhinoceros wanted to throw off the silly blanket. But it was so toasty under all the feathers that he couldn't do it. He found himself remembering how it felt to be a little baby, listening to his mother sing lullabies. To his surprise, he began to sing himself:

"Sleep little baby, so young and so new,
Nothing can bring you to harm.
I'll count the stars between Venus and Mars,
While you sleep safe in my arms."

It was the same lullaby Tilly's mother had sung to her.
She joined in on the second verse:

"Sleep little baby, so fresh and so fair,
Sleep in the woods, on the farm.
I'll sing a tune to the Man in the Moon,
While you sleep safe in my arms."

Now there is something magical about a goose and a rhinoceros singing together. When the lullaby was over, the two animals felt as if they had known each other a long time. They looked up at the frosty sky and counted the stars. They told hippopotamus jokes. The rhinoceros told Tilly that his name was Gregor, and she told him all

about her cottage and her work and her friends. They had such a good time that it was almost midnight when Tilly said goodnight and went home.

Gregor lay awake after she had gone, worrying because she wasn't

Two days later there was a snowstorm. When Tilly arrived with an extra-large feather hat for Gregor, she found him buried in a large drift. He looked very happy to see her. "What grows higher as it comes down?" he trumpeted hopefully.

"I wish I knew," Tilly sighed. "The truth is, Gregor, I am terrible at riddles."

"Oh, well," rumbled the rhinoceros. "Riddles aren't everything." All of a sudden he gasped, "Tilly! You've grown so tall!"

Tilly looked down. She was indeed towering over Gregor. "It's this snow," she explained. "It just keeps getting higher and higher."

"YES!" shouted the rhinoceros. "THAT'S IT! YOU'VE ANSWERED THE RIDDLE!"

"What do you mean, Gregor?" asked Tilly. "I didn't say anything."

But the castle bell began to peal, because the prince had overheard their conversation and knew the riddle was solved. Gregor climbed out of the drift. Even though it was snowing heavily, merchants began to arrive for the market laden with things to sell. In the midst of the excitement, Gregor went home with Tilly.

The next day the royal treasurer arrived at Tilly's cottage, with five hundred golden rubles and the key to the prince's extra castle and swimming pool.

Under Tilly's influence, Gregor became a delightful animal. He only asked riddles to entertain young children and told them the answers right away. He carried Tilly and her wares to market, and he carried her home again, and he saw to it that in winter she always wore galoshes over her webbed feet. Together they read to the sick, bandaged the wounded, and remembered the sad and lonely on Saint Valentine's Day.

When a rhinoceros is your friend, he is your friend for life.